VERSES KINDLER PUBLICATION

Kenisa Modi

Little Me, Big Dreams

Verses Kindler Publication

VERSES KINDLER PUBLICATION

Verses Kindler Publication.

Website: www.verseskindlerpublication.com

Little me, big dreams

By: Ms. Kenisa Modi

ISBN: 978-93-5605-854-5

FICTION STORIES 1st Edition

Price: 249 INR/$12

*To my Mummy and Pappa,
who knew I could do it.*

DISCLAIMER

Little me, big dreams is written by Kenisa Modi.

The published stories are the original contents of the author and the author has done her best to edit and make it plagiarism free.

The characters may be fictitious or based on real events but they are not meant to hurt anyone's feelings nor portray anything against any caste or system.

In case of any plagiarized write-up the author is solely responsible for it. The publisher would not be responsible for it.

Chapter One

JAINA NOBODY

Hey! I'm Jaina!

I'm a sixth grader at Green Hope Middle School. I'm a nobody at school. Middle School can be really tough. I just wished that I had friends in middle school. Not happening anytime soon. I guess nobody wants me because I'm Indian. There aren't a lot of people in middle school that are Indian.

American people pronounce my name as (jain-a), and my family pronounces my name as (jei-naa).

I always dreamed of being famous.

I am an author, artist, and baker. I can do it all. Just nobody notices those talents because I'm not that important.

The only people who have either noticed or appreciated my talents are my parents and my elementary school teachers. Here, in middle school, no one notices or appreciates my talents; not even the teachers notice!

Anyway, what I want my career to be is quite difficult to choose. But recently, I thought of becoming a doctor. All those talents can be either my side jobs or just hobbies.

This week is the third week of school, and to make it even worse, I had to go to my Aunt Charmi's house on the weekend since my parents had a bunch of errands to run. She's very old school. She's my dad's older sister.

My aunt is the type where everything must go her way. She's a terrible cook; she can't sew or knit, she can't draw, she can't do anything pretty much. All she can do is talk. Talk, talk, talk. I guess that's why she isn't married, and I think she'll never be.

But there was a time when my aunt was young and beautiful. She was very beautiful. I saw her old photos from when she was in college. But she never did any good. That's why nobody liked her. My dad told me when she was a kid, she refused to do any chores. All she did was sleep and eat. She got in a lot of trouble with their mom.
Now, my aunt wants me to be as spoiled as her. One time, when my parents called family members to celebrate my mom's birthday, I made a cake for her. When my aunt tasted the cake, she said it was terrible.
Dad said, "What are you talking about? This cake is amazing!"

Everyone started agreeing with him. My aunt got embarrassed. It was a sight to see!

In the third week of school, after my 7th period, I had 8th period, which was English.

English was my favorite subject. Miss. Samantha was nice but not nice enough to appreciate or notice my work. She liked to get work done faster. By the second week of school, we already started writing essays. We were supposed to start writing our essays in the fourth or fifth week of school.

So, after we came in, she started handing out pieces of notebook paper. Once she was finished handing out the pieces of paper, she announced that we were going to have a writing-a-poem contest.

Oh yeah! It's my time to shine! I could write any poem I wanted, too.

Most people hated poems. But I loved them! Especially the ones with rhyming words and couplets.

I wrote a funny poem about the ocean. I thought that this poem was the best poem I ever wrote!

When the time was up, Miss Samantha told us that she would call us to the front of the room to share our poems in 3 groups. The first group had 10 people, the second group had 10, and the third group also had 10. Then, we would all vote on the best one we liked.
I was super excited; I ended up being in the second group.

Alyssa read her poem about dogs first. Cameron read about football, then Celena read about reptiles, Milie read about flowers, Cora read about a lonely peacock, Nick read a very lousy poem about basketball, Max read about knights, Lily read about herself, Isabell read about princesses, and finally me. I read a poem about the ocean as it goes.

THE OCEAN

The Ocean is in motion
Which causes a commotion,
Where people throw potions,
Which causes explosions.

The fish in the ocean ring a bell,
For the well, they were trying to sell.

While the clams in the ocean,
Dwell a potion,
For they do not want an explosion,
For they do not want the ocean to break.

But when the ocean is in motion,
Which causes a commotion,
Where people throw potions,
Which causes explosions,
Which might cause implosions!

So don't harm the ocean,
If you want the ocean to be in motion!

Everyone thought my poem was the best. I got twelve votes including me, which was pretty good! So that meant I won! There were three winners: me, Sara, and Kelly!

I was so happy! Looks like I am somebody instead of nobody!

Chapter Two

LUNA

After that competition, Miss. Samantha gave me and the other two winners a gold ribbon that read the name in caps, then said "Great Poets!"

It was so cool!

Later that night, when I showed my parents the ribbon I got from school, they blew up in excitement. They promised me that we could go out to Olive Garden for dinner tomorrow.

WHOO-HOO! Win-win for me!

Early the next morning, I woke up and looked out my window. It was early morning around 5:50, so I could see the sun rising. It was so beautiful.

I could hear the birds chirping as the sun rose, up, up.
The sky was a beautiful orange and red, with a big shimmering yellow-orange circle in the center.
Behind our house, there was a humongous field. The field was still filled with white-tailed deer. There were also many trees, so that's where probably all the chirping was coming from.

After what felt like an hour, I went to the bathroom to take a shower.

I took a very long time in the shower. I like the warm water pounding against my skin. It feels really good.
Once I stepped out of the bathroom. I went downstairs to get my backpack ready for school so I didn't need to rush at the last minute. I had a bunch of time, it was only 7:00.

After 45 minutes, Mom exclaimed, "Jaina, the bus is here!"

"Coming!" I replied.

I quickly rushed to the front door, slung my backpack over my shoulder, and slid my feet into my sneakers as Mom unzipped my backpack and put my lunch in it.

"I packed your favorite, *Khaman*," says Mom.

"Thanks, mom. But I gotta go!" I say

"Have a good day!" she yells as I walk toward the bus. I go up the stairs, not making eye contact with the bus driver. Never make eye contact with the bus driver, or else she grunts at you and will think that you are very weird and start yelling at you. Once a boy on the bus looked into the eye of the bus driver. He was so terrified that he started going to school by car.

After I walked past the bus driver, I went to my regular spot, seat 20. I sat there alone as always.

As the next bus stop came by, the unexpected happened! A girl from my Math class came to me.

"Hola! I'm Luna!" she said.

"Hi, I'm Jaina", I said back.

"Is this seat available?" she asked.

"Yeah, it is available," I answered

"Thanks, amigo, nobody wants me in their seats" " she says.

"Same here", I say.
Luna and I talked on and on until we reached school. It felt like we were friends who hadn't met for a long time.

Luna told me that her mom was from Mexico and that her dad was from France. Unfortunately, her parents divorced when she was a little girl. Her dad lives in Chicago, Illinois. She can barely remember him and has never met him. She also said that sometimes it's hard for her mom to manage Luna and her younger brother all by herself. She also told me that her name meant the moon or light.

Her story is pretty sad.

After she told her story, I told my story. I told her that both my mom and dad were Indian, just from different areas. My mom was from Ahmedabad, Gujarat, and my dad was from Rajkot, Gujarat. My dad's dad passed away last year from cancer and my grandma is now all alone.

When we reached school, I went straight to homeroom where my homeroom teacher, Mrs. Evans, was waiting for me.

She smiled big and said, "Jaina! Congrats on winning the poem competition. Miss Samantha told me! I never knew you had such great talent!"

I chuckled and shrugged as if it was nothing. Mrs. Evans can get excited when a student does something nice or earns something. She always compliments them and says she's proud of you when she's not.

Anyway, we started our homeroom. Homeroom felt like five minutes.

Next was Science. I'm not piped up into science because everyone is taking ages on observing and observe a rock. We haven't even started the experiments yet. I think that the experiments are going to be boring too because nothing is interesting in rocks.
But the good thing is that Luna's going to be there. We can talk while everyone just experiments with those boring rocks.

When we reached the science classroom, our science teacher Mr. Kooper said, "Today we will do one more day of observation of the rocks. Then tomorrow we will share our notes, thoughts, and questions".

Great! Another day of observing. I hated observing rocks; I just had to find Luna.

I went to the back of the classroom to my usual spot and found Luna.

"Hey!" Luna said.

"Hi," I replied.
"Science is very boring, especially when we have only been observing rocks for days and days!" Luna exclaimed.

"I agree", I said. At least Luna and I had something in common.

For the rest of that period, Luna and I just talked about how science can be boring and stuff and what was going on in life besides school.

After school, when Luna and I were on the bus, a boy, Mac, who was in the seat in front of us, started to say, "I feel like I'm gonna throw up!"

Mac felt like throwing up, so his friend Nick moved out of his seat and moved to another seat.

Mac tried to hold it but eventually, he did throw up. It was disgusting, it was more of barfing. The stench was terrible. Girls were saying "EWWW!" and screaming boys were half laughing and saying "EWWW!" too.

But I had to agree the stench was terrible!

As soon as Mac's stop had come by, he ran out of the bus like a rocket.
I thought he was going to barf again and that he didn't want to barf on the bus again. But here's the problem: Mac sits in front of Luna and I and the throw-up is in front of us. That meant we had to hop from seat to seat to get off the bus.

I said goodbye to Luna and she did the same.

As soon as I got off, I started to skip home, but I didn't have to go all the way. Mom and Dad's car was near the bus stop. My mom waved and exclaimed, "Hop in! We're going to Olive Garden for dinner! But first, we're going to get ice cream!"

"Dad, you have to promise me that we'll get dessert after dinner!" I say.

"Okay fine!" Dad says.

"Oh, you won't believe what happened on the bus today. A kid threw up and we had to jump seats to get out of the bus!" I say.

"Ewww!" Mom cries out.

"That's exactly how everybody was", I reply. Mom and Dad started laughing, I joined in.

Chapter Three

DIARY DISASTER

Have I ever written a diary?

Yes, I have, and some of the diary entries have turned out to be a disaster.
The other day, I was cleaning out my room and found some boxes under my bed. They had all these diaries which I had written in them. I started looking at my first diary. I started writing them when I was about four years old. I didn't get the spelling right! My first diary took place on Saturday, July 3rd, 2017.

Dear Diaye

Today mom tuk me to ice ceem shop. I had fun. I got choclat ice ceem. Afer ice ceem, mom an me went shopinng. I sad to mom, I wunt thes buuk to wite. Mom sad yas. Now I wite in thes buuk abut my day. Mom wass hapy when shee saw my witing.

Dear Diaye

Today dad mom tuk me to road tip to Nee Yok Citee. I saw my aut. Mom dad leff me with aut. She was vewy mean. She cal me punny, tinny, an she sad nut to tuch anythung. Me was vewy saad.

Aut nut lef me du anythung. Me vewy bord. Su I wite in my buuk abut my day an my aut. Mom dad cam bak when dak. Then we wunt hom to seep. I big girl, so I seep alone. Butt, nut tooday.

Hahaha! Those two diaries make me laugh! Those were my good diary entrics. As I grew up, my diary entries became even better. The spelling did, too.

Dear Diaye,

Tumurrow is my birthday. I m turning sixx. I wil go tu fist grade an m vewy excited. Fur my birthday, I wunt a baking kut, cause I lik tu bake. My birthday paty wil be at a tampoline pak wit al my fiends. I cant wait! I wonda wat my fiends ar gonna give me fur my birthday. I hop it iz nut buuks. Big gownup buuks r boring. I thunk my aut wil be at my birthday paty. I dont wunt her tu be ther.

That was my birthday time. My aunt had come to my birthday party and she ended up giving me a grown-up book instead of a kid's book that I could read. Sometimes, for some diary entries, I wrote, FORGOT TO FINISH.

Dear Diary,

Today I went to a water park. I was in the car, driving to the water park, writing this diary. When we reached the water park, we went to the reception. The reception lady said two more hours till our room was ready. I couldn't wait! First we changed in the bathroom into our swimsuits, so we didn't have to wait for two more hours to get into the water.
Then we went down to the waterpark. The waterpark was humongous. I didn't know where to start. The good thing was that we were staying here for two days.

FORGOT TO FINISH

Sometimes, I didn't even finish the diary. Sometimes I wrote mad ones or sad ones. Happy and excited ones. I wrote a diary where I had the best time with my friend Ellie before I moved. Ellie and I had a playdate almost every single weekend. In the Summer, we used to have it every day!

That's how much fun we had.

Dear Diary,

Today, my friend Ellie's mom took Ellie and me to the movies to watch Hocus Pocus 2! We got sweet and salty popcorn with an icee (icee's are just slushies). I got a Coca-Cola flavored icee.

After the movie, we got to go to a local arcade to have lunch there and play a couple of games. I won 236 tickets in total. I had saved up all my tickets and had brought the tickets along. I checked the total and the total was 1,294 tickets. Ellie had done the same, her total was 1,047 tickets.

Ellie and I spent most of our tickets. I got a new diary, which is the one I am writing in now since my old diary is filled with stories and a cute panda keychain. Ellie got a donut squishy mellow and a unicorn keychain.

After that fun, we went home to relax and in the evening we all went to the pool!

THE END!

Sometimes, I wish I could go back and relive those moments.
But sometimes you can't.
I felt a little fresh after reading a couple, but then I found a diary entry that really made my day.

Dear Diary,

Today was my tennis competition. I was really nervous. My number was number 6. So I had plenty of time. I went to the court next to this one which was a practicing court. The court was empty, so I started slamming the wall with my tennis racket and tennis ball.

After some time, a girl from my team came to practice with me. We both played a mini-match. In the end, I won! We were just about to exit the court when the loudspeaker said, "Game Number 3 is OVER! Putting The Queens ahead!"

The Queens was our team name. For a while, all the girls in our team started to observe the other team's tactics. When it was my turn, I was so ready. Just let the game start and everyone can see me kill that girl.

I almost missed one of her shots but caught it quickly. I had put up The Queens in the lead by 1 more.

My next game was number 9, which came pretty soon. I was competing against the strongest girl in the team we were against. She was too fast. I missed some shots in the beginning but caught up in the end. I nearly got hit in the face and the ribs by the ball. But I still defeated her BAD!

Her face literally dropped when the loudspeaker said that I had one that matched. My whole team cheered. My mom treated everyone on our team to ice cream.

That night, we were the homecoming champions!

Chapter Four

SWIMMING SUCCESS

After reading those diaries, I was energized.
Like I joined the tennis team, I joined a swim team.
I had tried to join the Dolphins Swim Team for the winter season. I got selected and was going to have my second swim meet this Saturday. Swim meets are usually around 4 to 5 hours.

It was like a competition with another team. Swim meets are mostly and possibly always in the mornings. Some meets have a location that probably isn't local. Some can be super far, like an hour or forty minutes away, but sometimes, we have swim meets in the local pools, like the high school that's a mile away.

This week was going to be at that high school. I had to wake up at 6:30 since my swim meet was at 7:20. Well, not THE swim meet; it was just warm up, one last time of practice before competing.

I got my swim bag ready last night. I had put on my towel, extra goggles, caps, clothes, some soap, and a hair brush. I kept my blue and black swimsuit ready on my desk.

I wore my swimsuit and put on clothes on top. I packed a notebook and a strawberry milkshake that Mom quickly made for me. For breakfast, I had a banana.
Mom gave me a $10 bill in case I wanted to buy anything from the concession stand if I was hungry. Then she said, "Dad will drop you and come back. Then your dad and I will have breakfast and come right in time for your event."

"Okay, mom. Can you remind me of the events again?" I asked.

"Sure, let me check on my phone; it has your events on it", she replied.

She grabbed her phone from the counter and started tapping the phone screen. Then she said, "Event 22, 100 yard free, event 45, 50 yard back, event 54, 50 yard Breast, and Relay 70, 50 yard Free."

"Sounds good!" I say.

"Come on, kiddo, we're gonna be late for your warm-up!"

I quickly grabbed my bag, put on my flip-flops and rushed to the front door.

Then Dad drove me to the high school, took me to the pool, and said, "Okay, kiddo! Have fun!"

"Okay, Dad, I will!" I say.

He chuckles and turns around, heading toward the exit.
I took my place on the benches. I had packed two towels. I laid the first towel on the red bench that was for my butt. I placed my bag on the side and took off my flip-flops. At that time, the warm-up was starting. So I climbed down from the bench and jumped into the five-foot-deep pool. Then we started practicing. First, we did four laps of freestyle. Then we did two laps of butterfly, 2 laps of breaststroke, and 2 laps of backstroke. In the end, we did an 100 I.M.
100 I.M. is technically one lap of butterfly, one lap of breaststroke, one lap of backstroke, and one lap of freestyle. I was very excited.

In front of the red benches, there is a railing thing. On it, it had four of five papers that had your events, heats, relays, and what stroke I was supposed to do. In front of the railing was the practice pool. Beside the practice pool was the door to the high school hallway. There was a food stand right outside.

The high school is really big. It has a separate part for cultural arts and stuff. It has a huge pool, auditorium, and a basketball area, and the hall goes on forever!

After thirty minutes, event 19 had just started. The coaches all called the swimmers who were competing to form a line. Then she started calling out names, lining up people, and telling them what lane they were in.

I was in lane 3. Once the coaches were done telling our lanes, we rushed to get in line as they announced Event 20.

I really wanted my parents to make it to my event. Just as I was thinking that some familiar voice was shouting my name. I looked to the stands where the parents were sitting. I saw my parents standing and waving there. I waved back. They shouted, "You got this, Jaina!"

I know I got this.

When they announced event 21, the boy who was swimming in that event hopped out when there was a loud "beep!" At that moment, the girl in front of me climbed up the block and took her position.

Then a voice said, "Take your mark", and the girl lifted her hands into streamline. Then the voice yelled, "G.O.!" She dived down, down, down into the deep 13 feet waters. She made a huge splash. She was also swimming a 100-yard freestyle. She was the fastest of all.

She swam and swam all four laps and came in second place as her time 01. 23. 63.

She was really good.

When she reached the wall, she waited for the beep to climb up. When the beeper beeped, she climbed out, and I climbed the block and got into my position. I was really excited. I was sure that I wouldn't come last or first, but I would be close.

As the person who says things, the speaker said, "Take your mark," I raised my hands into a beautiful, long, and straight streamline.

I could smell the chlorine from underneath me. It was strong. I looked to my right and saw a girl who looked really nervous and weak; she was shivering. Then I looked to my left, and I saw a girl who was really ready. She had a blue swim cap, and strands of hair were coming out. I thought she had blonde hair. She was wearing a cute blue swimsuit with purple, light blue, baby pink, and white starfish. She hid her smile underneath her face.

When the person who says things to the speaker yells, "G.O.!" I dived smoothly down into the deep waters. I went down, down, down, then I went up, up, up, to the surface to take a breath. I took a quick breath and went back into the water again.
As I came up for my second breath, I glanced over to my left and saw that the girl was five yards away, and the girl to my right was a long way back.

As soon as I reached the wall, I did a flip-turn in the water, and I managed to touch the wall with two feet.
I then immediately came back to the surface and took another quick breath. I did the same for the other laps, too.

When I finished all four laps, I glanced over to the scoreboard and saw that I had made it to first place by 0.74 seconds. I was so happy!

On the way to the benches, Coach Emmy and Coach Gavin congratulated me and said, "Good job, Jaina! We're really proud of you!"

I gave them a "thanks and went to my spot on the red bench to wrap myself in a towel. Then, I saw my parents rushing over to the benches. I climbed down the benches with my strawberry smoothie in my hand and a towel wrapped around me.

"Good Job, kiddo!" Dad exclaimed.

"You were awesome out there!" mom cried out.
"Can you believe that you beat the girl just by 0.74 seconds?" Dad says.

"Yes, Dad, I know that," I say. "I'm just going to grab something from the food stand".

"Okay, Jaina, we'll be in the stands", said Mom.

"Okay," I say as my parents turn around and walk out.
I walked over to the food stand as soon as my parents left. I looked at the small menu they had, and everything was $1 or $2. chose to get a glazed donut, which was $

I pulled out my $10 bill and gave it to the person who was running the food stand. He gave me the glazed doughnut and then started getting the change. Once he found the change, which was $8, he handed it to me and bid farewell.

After all my events, I had my relay. The coaches called down the swimmers who would be swimming in that relay.

"Lilianna, Jaina, Olivia, and… Let's see Victoria," announced the coach.

Everyone came down the benches except Victoria. She wasn't even on the benches! Our relay was soon, and if Victoria didn't show up, we couldn't compete in the relay. I really wanted to compete in the relay this time.
Last time, a girl, Sophie, was sick and missed the whole swim meet, so we couldn't do the relay.

This time, I wanted to do the relay really badly.
The coach started asking us, "Have any of you seen Victoria?"

Olivia shot up her hand and exclaimed, "I have! She was competing against me for event 18!"

"Oh, yes! I remember!" said the coach. "But has anyone else seen her after?"

I raised my hand and asked the coach, "Do you have a picture of Victoria? I can't remember what she looks like."
"Oh, of course!" says the coach.

She pulled out a picture from her bag and handed it to me. That picture was from picture day. The coach takes her finger, which just looked like it had a manicure, and points it to the third row, where a beautiful blonde-haired girl is kneeling down. She was also wearing a starfish swimsuit. She looked like the same girl whom I was competing against at event 22.

I gave the picture back and thought, what if she had a twin? What if I was just seeing things, and this girl just had the same swimsuit as the one I was competing against? I finally made up my mind.

"Yes, I have seen her!" I exclaimed. "She was competing against me; she was really good!"

"Yes, she is one of our best, but have you seen her after that?" Now the coach was going to lose it. Her voice seemed like it was going to burst, but she was holding it.

Everyone shook their heads.

The coach groaned, turned around and stomped away, murmuring words under her breath.

Chapter Five

FIGHTING BACK CHILDHOOD FEARS

All the girls in my relay decided to split up and start looking for Victoria.

Liliana went to search near the food stand. Olivia went to search where all the parents were seated. I went to search the girls' bathroom/lockers.

The girls locker room was next to the trophies which swimmers have won. I pushed open the door to the locker room. The locker rooms were humongous!

I walked through the bathrooms first, where I saw all the bathroom stalls open with no one in them.

I took a look at the sinks; they sure were dirty!

Next, I walked over to the locker rooms where I saw a lot of lockers. The lockers were all around, like it was blooming like a flower. I looked through every single locker that I could open. I found no one.

Then I turned to go to the big shower room. The shower room was empty just as I heard a voice.

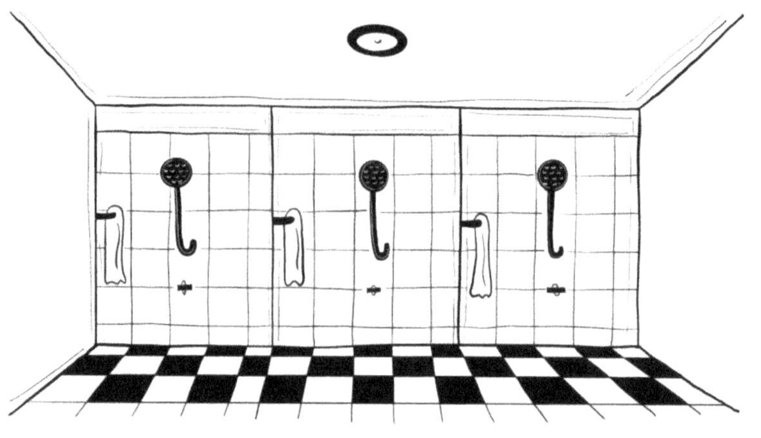

"What are you doing here?" a girl asked.

I turned around to see Victoria.

"Victoria!" I exclaimed. "You have to hurry! Our relay is about to start!"

Victoria shifted her feet and rocked back and forth.

"What's wrong?" I ask.

"I - It's just that I'm a bit nervous," she said. "I think I want to sit this one out."

"NO!" I cried. "Oh, uh, sorry. But you can't miss out on this relay. If you don't compete with us, then surely we'll lose. I saw you compete against me; you were really good!"

"Not as good as you," she groaned. "You beat me."

"Oh come on, tell me the truth, is something bothering you?" I ask her, listening carefully for an answer.

"Okay, I think I can tell you," she said as I eagerly waited for her answer. "I am right about me being nervous, but there is another thing. I - I… " she hesitated. "I have a childhood fear of water. My parents made me go swimming. I don't enjoy it all! All they care about is me being successful- way too successful. They named me Victoria because it means Victory."

"Oh, I see," I say. "But you're a strong swimmer; how can you still be afraid?"

"Because I have a fear of water," she says. "My parents used to be swimmers, too. Now they want me to follow their path."

I couldn't believe that one of our greatest swimmer on the team was being forced to swim by her parents. Let alone, she had a fear of water!
I had to find a way to calm her down and get her to compete with us.

At that moment, the loudspeaker announced, "For Relay 67, we have the girl's 50-yard freestyle with Willamson, Campbell,

Collins, and Miller competing against…" It went on and on, saying all the girls' last names.

"Listen," I say. "You can't be afraid!"

"How?" Victoria asks.

"We don't have to win or lose; the main thing is that we should try," I said.

Victoria sighed, "I guess you're right."

She stood up. I did the same. Then she marched straight out of the locker rooms and the bathrooms. She marched up to the pool in front of our coach and said, "I'm here!"

"Ahh, Victoria, hurry! The relay is about to start!" the coach cried out.

The coach quickly numbered us and told us which lane we were all supposed to go in.

As we rushed to our lane, the loudspeaker announced relay 69. We were just in time for our relay!

As soon as relay 69 was over, Victoria stepped up on the block.

The loudspeaker shouted, "Ready…. GO!"

Victoria dived into a streamline and went down, down, down.

The rest of our teammates and I were shouting and screaming, "GO VICTORIA!"

She was super fast!

When Victoria got onto her second lap, the other girl in the lane next to Victoria on the right was almost done with her first lap. The girl on the left was a little ahead of Victoria, just a little.

When Victoria completed her two laps, I was already on the block and dived above Victoria's head and into the water, going down, down, down. Then, when I was running out of breath, I swam up, up, up to the surface.

I swam and swam until I reached the wall.

I pushed off the wall and continued swimming as fast as I could.

I started to feel a little tired when I came closer to the wall. It was only a couple of yards away. I was almost there…

I made it to the wall, and Olivia dived over the top of my head. So far, we were in the lead!

The same process happened one more time. Liliana was a bit slow; after all, she was the youngest on our team. But Liliana touched the wall a second before anybody else could. That meant we won!

Chapter Six

IT'S DIWALI!

Diwali is right around the corner, and I am really nervous.

I honestly just wish to fly away and disappear on that day. Sure, you will get a couple of bucks and a present from your parents, maybe. Sure, you can get sweets and more sweets all the time.

But the fireworks and the lamps, uh uh.

Doesn't anybody realize how dangerous it is for kids to be lighting up fireworks and lamps?

I really don't like Diwali.

On Saturday, my mom searched her closet for my Indian dresses.

"It has to be here somewhere," she said.

"Mom, you know what, forget about it. I'll just wear something simple," I say. But that was a mistake!
"No!" mom exclaimed. Ba sent it to you, especially for Diwali. She bought really nice dresses from India, and she even bothered to courier them to us, and you're not going to wear them?"

I just stared at her in disbelief. I knew that my ba or should I say, my grandma, always sends dresses for special occasions, and everytime, my mom makes me wear the dresses.

Sometimes the dresses are just so uncomfortable! They can get so itchy and heavy.

"Uhmm…" I stuttered. "Actually, I changed my mind. I will wear the dresses."

"Good," Mom turned back to the box and started rummaging in for my dress. If I had said no, she'd go crazy again.

When she found it, she held it up and turned to me.

"Do you like it?" she asked.
The dress was a beautiful dress. It had the colors light pink, lavender, dark purple, and blue, all shaded in on the bottom of the dress. The dress also came with a light pink and purple dupatta.

"Uhm, I have one question," I say.

"Yes?" Mom asks. "Go ahead."

"Is the dress, uhm uh…" I stuttered, afraid that she might go crazy again if I asked that question.

"Is the dress itchy?" My mom asked the question for me. "Well, the answer to that question is, why don't you find out yourself?"

I groaned. Great! I had to try out the dress to see if it was itchy or not.

Mom held up the dress in front of me happily and I grabbed it, slowly walking to the bathroom with a face that didn't look happy.

I could hear Mom laugh as I closed the bathroom door.
I didn't even bother to take off my shirt. I just pulled it straight up; that way, I wouldn't have to feel the itchiness.
I swung the dupatta over my shoulder and opened the door with a dull face. Mom looked at me in disbelief.
She started to laugh and cried out, "What are you wearing?" She was still laughing. She was laughing and laughing, and I just looked at her, laughing and laughing until she was finally done.

"I put on what you told me to put on, "I said.

"Oh, here, let me help you!" Mom said.

Finally, after what felt like an hour trying out new dresses and jewelry, Mom said we were going out for dinner in this new Italian restaurant. The name was complicated.

I was guessing it was in Italian.

The restaurant had opened yesterday, so there was a large crowd waiting in line for their tables.

"Uh oh," I whispered so only mom could hear.

"No, Jaina, we aren't going to have to wait in that humongous line." Mom said, pointing towards the line.

"I made a reservation last week."
"Last week?" I asked.

"Yup, the restaurant was allowing that," she said.

"Huh, that's smart," I say.

Mom chuckles and walks over to the counter where Dad is standing and waiting.

The woman behind the counter asked, "Do you have any reservations?" and then gave Mom a wink.
"Yes," Mom said, giving her a wink, too. "It's under the name Priya."

The woman behind the counter nodded and started tapping some buttons on the iPad that seemed glued to the counter; then, she said, "Ahh, I see your name. Right this way."

The woman called for a lady named Kelly, who I guess was our waitress.
Kelly immediately showed up and grabbed three menus from the counter and turned to us to say, "follow me, I'll show you your table."

We walked straight until we found ourselves turning a corner on the right and then going up a spiral staircase. We found ourselves on the top floor looking at an indoor garden with a couple of tables and a bar.

I looked at Mom in astonishment.

Mom smiled and gestured for me to sit down on the decorated table.

The waitress, named Kelly, said, "Hello, I am Kelly, and I will be servicing you for this dinner. If you'd like to order anything, you can press this button, and one of us will come by." She pointed to the green button on the wall.

"Thank you," dad said.

Kelly turned around and started going down the spiral staircase.

I looked around to see the tables filled with people. It was a good thing Mom got a reservation for this table last week.

"Now, to answer your question," said Dad. "We got the beautiful garden on the top floor because…"
Dad waited for a second, and then Mom answered for him, "We own this restaurant!"
"What?!" I exclaimed. "That's amazing!"
I couldn't believe it. For a moment, I felt confused, but now I was so excited!

"Could I help here on the weekends?" I asked.

"Sure," Dad said.

Two more days until Diwali. I'm so nervous.

My cousins were going to visit us for Diwali. They don't live too far; they live in Greensboro, North Carolina. Just three hours away from us.

It turned out that they were going to stay for 3 days: Saturday, Sunday, and Monday. I have three cousins. One is in 5th grade, the second is in 2nd grade, and the last one is six months. Diwali was on Sunday, and mom said to make cards to give to my cousins for Diwali. I didn't understand the point of cards. If I give it to my younger cousins, what are they going to do with it? They can't read it. My cousin who is the oldest is very careless, probably going to throw it away.

I could argue with Mom, but there's no point; she'll make me do it anyway.

That day, during lunch at school, I took some paper, some markers and coloured pencils and started making three cards for my cousins.

I decided to draw a *diya.* Diya is basically a lamp. We light them up for Diwali, the Festival of Lights.

On the back of the card, I wrote *Happy Diwali!*

When I finally finished making the cards, I decided to go downstairs to get a little snack. I was lucky that my science teacher hadn't given me much homework; she always gave me so much homework. The rest of the teachers give little homework, I mostly finish that during the break that we get everyday. It's like a work period where you can do whatever you want to do. But most of the time, I use it to finish homework.

Waiting, waiting, waiting…

We were waiting for my cousins to arrive. They're supposed to come at 11. It's 11:30. Dad says that there was some traffic and they will be here around 12.

Great.

My mom was starting to make lunch. She was planning to make puri and Indian gravy potatoes. She also was going to make Kesar mango rus. Kesar mango rus is like mango mushed in a blender with a little water and kesar and blah, blah, blah.

We could make all that except the Kesar mango rus. Dad forgot to buy them from the grocery store.
"Jaina," mom said. "Go and get 5 big mangos from Auntie Antina."

Auntie Antina is one of our family friends; she lives a block away on Grape Street.

Mom gave me a small lemon-yellow cloth bag to carry the mangos.

I stepped out of the house and walked across the street. I reached house 107 and ding-donged the doorbell.

Auntie Antina opened the door almost immediately, as she knew I was coming.

"Ah, beta, how are you?" asked Auntie Antina.

"I'm good, Auntie; what about you?" I replied.

"I'm all good," says Auntie Antina. "What brings you here?"

"Oh, I'm just here to collect five big mangos," I say.
"Ahhh, I see, having guests? Mom sent you, didn't she?" she
says, I nod. "Come inside, sit down, it might take me a while."

I entered her beautifully decorated living room. She has a
humongous couch in the middle with big, small average plants
surrounding the room. There were pictures hung here and there.
There was a large TV above the fireplace.

Auntie Antina went down the hallway to the kitchen to get the
mangos.
As I was sitting, I heard footsteps coming down the stairs. I
thought it was Krish, Auntie Antina's son, but it turned out it
was Uncle Rohan.

"Jaina!" he boomed. "Long time no see!"

"Yes, uncle," I say as I stand up.

Uncle Rohan, Auntie Antina and Krish moved to Jamestown,
Virginia, six months before us. I chuckle, then ask, "Where's
Krish?"

"He must be at one of his friend's houses, always roaming
around," he says.

I nod when Auntie Antina comes with a basket with five large
mangos.

"I got some mangos!" She sings. She drops the mangos into my bag.

I thank them and say bye. I haul the heavy mangos onto my hands and slowly walk toward home, struggling to carry them.

What? I'm not a weightlifter!
As I open the door and walk towards the kitchen, Mom is waiting for me. She looked like she had to wait a long time, and she definitely did not look happy.

"Well, that took you long enough," she says with both hands on her hips.

I know what to do in these situations: DON'T talk.
"The Diwali presents are in my closet, along with some wrapping paper for gifts. Go gift wrap them."

I nod and haul myself up the stairs. I go down the hall and go into the master bedroom. I walk toward the closet and flick on the light. I see a target bag and some gift wrapping paper. I take them out of the closet and sit down while also setting the target bag on the floor too.

The first thing that comes into my hand is a Skipper Babysitting Barbie. Mom put a sticky note on it that says, "Zara", in her beautiful cursive handwriting, the one in sccond grade. I take the sticky note off and take the pink with white strips of wrapping paper. I cut the wrapping paper in half because it was way too big.

I started wrapping the Skipper Babysitting Barbie Set by putting the set in the middle and then putting the paper on top of the set. It's complicated.

I hold the paper with one hand while grabbing some tape from the other and taping it on. I then take a sharpie and write *Zara.*

I will use the same process for the other gifts. Kushi, the fifth grader, got an art kit since she loves art like me. Trisha, the six-month-one, she got, well, baby stuff. What else would she get?

I finished wrapping all the gifts and put them away in mom's closet. Mom called me down and told me she got a call from our Masa or uncle. They were two minutes away.

She poured four glasses of water and put them on a tray.

Just then, the doorbell rang, "ding, ding, ding, dong!" Somebody was dinging it too many times.

Dad answered the door and announced, "*Avo, avo*, welcome." My Masa and Masi or my aunt and uncle enter. Mami has sleeping Trisha in her hands. Zara was awake and energetic and Kushi was in the middle.

"Come sit," gestured my mom as she brought the tray of water. Dad took in their luggage.

"It has been a long time since I met you, brother.

Despite you living so close, you never come to visit," says Masa.

"Well, what can we do? You guys should have come too?" says Dad.

"We didn't want to bother you," says Masa.

"Oh, don't worry about that. Anyway, lunch is ready, so whenever you're ready, we can have lunch," says Mom.

"Sure, we can have it now. Ajay, can you get the blanket from the car?" says Masii.

"Let me show you your bedroom," says Mom. Masi, Zara, Trisha, Kushi and Mom go upstairs.

"Here, let me help you," says Dad to Masa.
So, today's Diwali. I am already starting to dislike it. Masi brought chocolate for Diwali, so Kushi, Zara, and I started eating them all up. One thing I like.

Early in the morning, we all wore traditional Indian clothing and did some pooja.
Pooja is like praying to the god, singing some songs, and etc.

The thing that I'm most scared about is the night… I wish it would never come. Once Pooja was done, Masa got me a gift. He gave me a giant 1000+ piece lego set. I'm going to have fun building it.

In the afternoon, we watched a movie and played with Trisha. Every second gets me closer and closer to the night.

It's finally evening, the thing I most dreaded for.
I was there to see the sunset, and then I started worrying.

"Mom?" I groaned. Mom looked in my direction. "Can I go to sleep early?"

"No!" it was a straight up no from mom. "You are going to experience the fireworks today, next time, and whenever we do fireworks. Understand?"

"Fine, understand."

No. I didn't understand, and I didn't want to understand.
I went upstairs and found Trisha and Masi playing on the bed. Zara was with them, drawing or doing something in her notebook.

I went to my room and found Khushi on the bed reading a book, The Untouchables, by Gordon Korman. Me and Kushi shared a room together. Zara, masi, and Masa slept on the bed in the guest bedroom. Trisha slept in an old crib we still had.

"Hi," said Kushi in her quiet voice, pulling out an earbud from her left ear. "Sorry, I didn't see you."

"It's okay," I say. "But time for fireworks."
"Oh, okay, coming!"

I go into the guest bedroom and call Masi down for the fireworks. Here we go! The thing I dreaded the most is finally here.

Chapter Seven
FIREWORKS

Fireworks!

It's time, and I'm really not excited. But I know who is, Zara.

I don't really get how excited Zara can be. Kushi isn't really excited because she has already experienced it and has no problem with them. I have experienced them but I still don't like or enjoy them. It's weird how I, the older one, dislikes fireworks, other than somebody younger than me who enjoys and is cool with fireworks.

In the garage, my dad took out the large and small sparklers. Masi and Mom got matches and a lamp to light the fireworks with.
We were going to start the Diwali fireworks, which was the worst part.

Once we finished the sparklers, which I think wasn't the worst part, we moved on to the big fireworks. Zara was so excited that she was jumping up and down and squealing her head off. We were doing fireworks on the big road, near the field in front of our house.

I was really nervous and asked Mom to go to the bathroom as an excuse.

"NO," a straight-up no from Mom. She knows it's an excuse.

"Jaina, how can you be scared of fireworks? Nothing has happened to you so far," says Masi. "Look at these two." She points to Zara and Kushi, jumping up and down, begging Dad and Masa to hurry up.

I take a deep breath and sigh.
Once Dad put the fireworks in the right place, he took the lamp from Mom's hand and walked over to the box that contained the fireworks. Then he lit it up, and the box lit up in flames in no time.

Dad stepped back and watched. I stood on our patio, watching from a distance. It was a chilly night with the moon hidden behind the clouds. I cuddled up in my soft jacket.

The firework came out immediately, flipping the box upside down and dousing the small flame.
The firecracker shot up into the dark, clear sky and exploded into tiny, tiny, colorful bits.
Okay, that wasn't that bad, but the others could be worse.

My dad called me over, and I hurried to him. "You're lighting the next one." He had a real stern look on his face, and I started whining like a little four-year-old.
"You're doing it, whether you like it or not; you do this every year."

Now, I knew if I wasn't going to listen, then I was going to get in trouble. I took the firework box and lamp, marched over to the black, withering box and placed the box next to the used box.

I shivered, and my teeth chattered.

I slowly took the lamp toward the box and made sure that the lamp's fire touched the wax stick. Immediately, it burst into a tiny flame. That scared me, and I was sure I fell on the road. I got up immediately and dusted myself off.

I could hear snickering behind me. I turned around to see Kushi, Zara, Masi, and mom were snickering. Dad and Masa just had a smile on their face that could break into a chuckle any second.

I ran back with the lamp still in my hand, trying not to douse the flame. Then I took my place next to mom and saw the fireworks shoot into the sky, making a very loud ear-splitting sound. Louder than the last one.
Just then, Auntie Antina, Uncle Rohan, and Krish walked onto our street just in time to see the fireworks. Turns out, they were going to shoot fireworks into the air with us, plus they brought more fireworks.

This night was going to be a long one.

Chapter Eight
BIG DREAMS

"THUMP! THUMP! THUMP!" my books, notebooks, and everything else in my bag were moving up and down, right to the left, weighing me down. My legs were aching with pain as I made another right onto Avery Way, hauling my bag on my back and trying to keep the straps on my back as I walked.

Teachers give a lot of unnecessary stuff and say, "You must keep it in your bag; you may never know when you need it!"

It's the beginning of the year; if this keeps up, imagine how much they will give in the middle of the school year. Another "THUMP!" came as I tried to keep up my bag. I'm almost there, I think.

Thanksgiving weekend was finally here after loads of waiting. The school feels like it's there forever. A week feels like half a month, and the weekend feels barely like a day! So when I get home, I'm going to fling my backpack on the side of the sofa, grab a snack and watch TV.

Yeah, that sounds like a good plan to me! But unfortunately, fate had other plans for me.
Mom and Dad were planning a trip to go somewhere for vacation for a couple of days. I wasn't planning to go anywhere on Thanksgiving weekend. I tried to sit down and watch TV, but I couldn't get over the ruckus of where my parents were

deciding on where to go. I wish they had asked me, but no one ever does.

If they had asked me, my answer would have been very simple: whale watching. I've always wanted to go since I was a little kid. My parents and I were watching a whale movie, and if this is correct, the character went whale watching and had amazing adventures, and that's when I decided that I wanted to go whale watching.

Now it's November, and it might be cold, but the weather gave us mercy and decided not to make it chilly yet.

If anybody asked me, 'If you could, where would you go around the world?' Without hesitation, I would have said whale watching. Not Paris in France, nor Venice in Italy. Not Sydney in Australia, nor Moscow in Russia. Not Beijing in China, nor Rio de Janeiro in Brazil.

All I wanted to do was to go whale watching anywhere.

Now, well, since my parents were making such a ruckus in the other room, I decided to go up to my room and read a nice book. Maybe I can finish a couple of books this long, Thanksgiving weekend.

I decided to read the new book I got a couple of months ago, *Restart.*

Restart is about this kid named Chase, who's a jerk/bully who unfortunately fell off his roof and got amnesia (memory loss). Now, he has forgotten everything and is turning into a good guy. That's how far I got until my parents called me down.

I hurried down the wooden steps and entered the dining room, where my parents were discussing where to go.

"So, Jaina," said Dad. "We couldn't think of any place to go, and if we did, it wouldn't work out."

"Okay," I say, seeing where this is going. "So what do you want me to do?"

"Well," Mom says in a sing-song voice. "We were planning to let you pick the destination."

"Aren't you guys already guessing where I am thinking of going?" I asked, surprised that they hadn't thought of whale watching.

"I think I forgot about where you always wanted to go," Dad said nervously, fake chuckling and running his hand through his hair.

I put my right hand on my hip and said, "Ha-ha, very funny. I want to go whale watching!" Mom and Dad plastered a wicked smile on their faces. They looked so evil!

"Done!" said Mom.

Chapter Nine

BALWINDER UNCLE'S HOUSE

The next day, we were ready to go whale watching!
Dad said that we were planning to stay at one of his friend's houses, which lives near Cape Lookout, the place we are going to.

Cape Lookout is just a six-and-a-half-hour drive. I decided to bring three books for the road trip. Dad said we were planning to stay there for two or three days. Mom told me that the place where we're going to stay (my dad's friend) and the person who lives there (my dad's friend) are amazing artists.

Well in that case, I'll get to see some art on our trip. I started to read a book called *Red Queen*. *Red Queen* is about this poor girl who met this boy who looked like a red (blood type) but actually was a sliver (higher class) and a prince. He got the girl a job at the palace saving her life from not going to war. Then she figures out that she has powers and stuff and strange things happen in the palace to her.

I was in chapter nine when Dad pulled over to get some gas. I looked at the GPS map in the front and saw that we had four hours left. Great! I'm really not fond of long car drives.

I decided to take a break from reading and look outside the window as Dad stepped inside the car and stepped on the pedal. I looked at the sign at the gas station sign before Dad left the station. It said *Suffolk, Virginia.*

After what seemed like 10 hours, we came to a stop. I looked outside to see an elegant brick and stone house. The street looked beautiful, with giant, full-grown oak trees lined up on the sides of the street. The road looks new and sleek.

Dad pulled the vehicle up to their driveway and parked it there. Dad, Mom who had been mostly asleep during the trip here, and I stepped out of the car and we all stretched because our muscles had been asleep. I nearly tripped as I stretched. My muscles had really been sleeping and they were going to let me down, literally.

Dad ding-donged the doorbell and nobody answered for a while. Dad pressed the doorbell again and I could hear the pounding of footsteps get louder and louder as they came closer and closer to the door.

A man with a stubby beard and curly mustache answered the door, and a skinny woman with a close-to-dirty apron was propped behind.

"Namaste, namaste pah-ji!" bellowed the man and hugged Dad. He was speaking Punjabi, and I could tell that he was saying, 'Hello, my friend!'

The skinny woman came up to Mom and hugged her, too; she muttered something to Mom, and Mom muttered something back to her. We entered the warm and cozy home with a large living room near the door. The skinny woman hurried into the kitchen while the man seated us down on the rough couch.

The skinny woman swayed into the room with a tray of large cups.

"Ahhh, here's the *lassi!*" shouted the man.
The skinny woman came up to Mom and Dad and gave them large steel glasses filled with mango lassi. I was the last one she came up to.

She handed me a very heavy glass and muttered, "Namaste, beta. I don't think we have met before… I am Kajol auntie." She whispered so quietly that I could barely hear her.
I nod and sip the sweet, cold mango yogurt drink. The drink was so cold, I thought my teeth turned into small ice cubes. Dad boomed over my thoughts and said,
"Balwinder, it's been so long, my friend!" Mom and Kajol auntie giggle.

"Jaina, did you know that Balwinder uncle and dad were childhood friends from when they were really young," said Mom. Balwinder uncle scooched up to me and put a big, hairy, and heavy arm around my shoulder.

"Jaina, there are so many stories of me and your dad; I should tell them all to you," he boomed. I slightly nodded my head.

"You're a quiet little girl, not like your dad, who used to talk a lot!" he boomed again. I plastered a small, fake smile.

Oh great!

Chapter Ten

WHALE WATCHING, HERE WE COME! (OR NOT...)

The next day, we left at ten in the morning to Cape Lookout.

We left half of our luggage at Dad's crazy friend's house. Dad forecasted that today would be a great day to go Whale Watching. Cape Lookout was about 2 hours away.

Mom let me watch a movie on the iPad since I was already so bored. I went into NETFLIX and clicked the downloads button. A list of shows and movies popped up. I scrolled through the list and finally found Wednesday Addams.

I clicked on the show and started to rewatch the show for the third time. Wednesday Addams is amazing, just the monster's eyes are creeping me out.

I reached the third episode when dad pulled up. I turned the iPad off and sat straight up looking at the window. Cape lookout had the sun shining all over the place, pouring all the warmth on us. A couple of cars were pulled up. Dad took us to the big building and I looked at the cars. I could tell how many seats were in the car.

A black 7-seater Mercedes.

A small silver Honda.

A silver Mercedes Van with 12 seats.

And a large orange Ford truck.

Wow, looks like everyone wanted to come today.

Dad pulled us into the large elegant building with sea animals sculpted into the walls with seashells and coral too.

A large argument was happening inside. Dad told Mom and me to wait out here while he slipped into the crowd. People were yelling (well, not yelling), and it seemed like the crowd wanted something that the people in this building took away.

Dad slipped out of the crowd and, a couple of minutes later, with a sorry look on his face.

"I'm sorry Jaina, but all the boats for whale watching are not available. The next time they are available is after Thanksgiving break," he muttered.

"Oh," I whispered. So it looks like no whale watching at all. We have to head back to Dad's crazy friend's house. It takes about two hours to get there. Why did we come here in the first place?

"Maybe another time," said Mom, rubbing my back.

I was so looking forward to this trip, but now, we'll have to come back home or probably somewhere else…

Chapter Eleven

"WHOOP!"

We were on our way to Balwinder Uncle's house, and I felt like doing nothing except reading. I read and read until I finished the book. I looked over at the GPS and looked at how many hours we had left.

Thirty minutes more of driving! That'll feel like an eternity to me.

"*SCREECH...*" The car swooped to the left side of the road and stopped. Dad muttered under his breath, probably cursing.

He got out of the car and kneeled down in front of one of the car tyres. After some time, he opened the car door and said, "*A coy gadi ne takeni nay!*" Which meant that he practically cursed at the car.

My mom put a hand on his shoulder to calm him down.

"*Thies minutes dur che.* We'll call Balwinder," said my mom. She was right, it was thirty minutes away from Balwinder Uncle's house. But what I didn't get was what was the point of calling Balwinder uncle? My dad seemed to feel the same way, but it seemed like he understood half of it.

"We can call Balwinder, but what will happen to this car? It will cost a lot for the tow truck. There are not many tow trucks around the area."

My mom nodded and said, "*Balwinder ne phone karo*, maybe he can help?"

My mom was not giving up on calling Balwinder uncle, and my dad sensed it, too.

"Fine, *phone kar,*" said dad, finally giving in to call Balwinder uncle. My mom dug through her purse and then pulled out her phone. She dialed Balwinder Uncle's number and handed the phone to Dad.
My dad stepped out of the car and talked to him while my mom sighed. I knew this was going to be a long day. I decided to take out my notebook and write a small story. I always wondered what it would be like to be an author. I always had wild stories built up in my head. I just didn't write them down. It would take too long for the story to be written onto a piece of paper.

I pulled out my notebook with beautiful blood-red roses on it. Mom didn't like it, but this is what I asked for for my birthday. It looked really pretty, and I wrote small stories in it. It was only for my stories, and that's it.

I rapped my pencil on my head, trying to think of a story. I would write the summary down first so I don't make any big changes in the middle of the story or have to erase part of the story to include something else. I hated doing that, so I started writing down summaries before writing the actual story. I never really completed one story before because I was always too lazy or got bored.

My head started hurting and I realized that I was rapping the pencil too hard. I decided to go with an old story I had in the back of my mind. I pressed the pencil tip to the paper and started writing. I wasn't going to decide on names yet. I would fix that later. This story took place way back when there were all the King's and Queen's ruled.

I started writing the story.

'In this story, there is a girl who lives in a small house with her one older brother, one younger sister, one younger brother, and their mother. Their father was lost at sea, and the mother was doing everything she could to keep her children from harm. The family lived near the ocean, and almost every day, the girl would go by the shore and sit there. Her world was trapped; her mother wanted her to get married, but she didn't want to get married. She only said yes for the family's betterment. There were soldiers all over the place, and they weren't allowed to do anything except work. Every day, the girl wished she could soar high like the beautiful birds in the sky, free from everything. She would fly and fly until she got tired. She'd rest and sleep, but then she would be back up in the sky, soaring and flying high. But that all was a dream. She knew that wasn't possible. Once a year, there is a festival at the town square, and the girl and her family go. They went this year too.', I wrote. I tried to think what I should write next.

By now, Dad was inside the car again, talking with Mom, but I zoned out. I was too focused on the summary for some reason. I always wanted to write a story that was both emotional and fierce.

'This year, the prince and the princess were going to come to the festival. When they arrived, dirt and rock flew everywhere. It was a bomb. In all the chaos, the family was separated. The girl looked everywhere for her family, but she couldn't find them. She saw the royal prince and princess being escorted away. Selfish, she thought. Another bomb sounded, and the girl panicked and shouted for her mother and siblings. She found her mother, and the mother told her to find her siblings. The girl didn't want to be left alone, but she had to agree to find her siblings.
'She heard soldiers marching but couldn't tell if they were the soldiers to fight for us or against us. She ran and ran, shouting for her brother and sister. She didn't want to lose them. People screamed and ran all around her. She found her mother in an open field, holding onto her younger brother. She was backing away. She couldn't tell why her mother was backing away. She ran toward her and then stopped in her tracks. It was the enemy. The enemy soldier was holding a big gun pointed towards her mother. The girl screamed and ran toward the soldier. The other enemy soldiers raised their guns, but the soldier who held the gun pointed towards her mother pulled the trigger. Before you know it. The mother was gone. Her younger brother was scared, and the girl was forced to the ground. They threatened her and then were ready to pull the trigger when a sword met the enemy soldier's neck, and his head was immediately detached from his body. The girl screamed but then realized who had saved her and her brother. Her brother gasped. It was the prince. Not everyone got to meet the royals. Some people

would fall on their feet. But the girl didn't care. She wouldn't bow or clean his feet.
'The prince helped the girl up, and the girl ran with her younger brother, who was holding her hand. She ran and ran. She ran to the beach. She couldn't find her older brother and sister. She hoped that they hadn't met the same fate as her mother did. She sat there and mourned with her brother about her mother's death. There was nothing she could do.'

Now, my hand started to hurt, and I smiled. It was a good start so far. This took up three pages in my notebook, and I shook my hand, trying to get rid of the pain. I sighed and admired my work. This was good enough so far. This could be four or five chapters.
I wanted to write more, but I was tired.

"Okay," I heard Dad say from outside of the car. "You and Jaina can go with Balwinder while the mechanic arrives."
Mom nodded and looked at me, "Come on."

Chapter Twelve

PAV BHAJI

We finally reached Balwinder uncle's house.

Balwinder uncle had come to pick us up while the mechanic took his time and arrived late evening that day.

I was exhausted and just wanted to fall onto a bed and sleep for a hundred years. She was exhausted from sitting in a car and driving to places that felt like they were ten hours away. She was exhausted from being pushed around places. It was dark when we arrived, and I was about to sit on the sofa when Kajol auntie rushed into the room, stopped me and pointed a finger at the table.

Or at least where the table should have been.

The table was covered with wood and dust. I looked up at the roof and saw that there was a small open patch on the roof.

"Oh," mom gasped. "What happened?"

"Well," Kajol auntie began. "This morning, just after you left, it started raining hard. So…". She looked up at the roof and shook her head slowly. "ise vaise bhee theek karane kee jaroorat thee. Mujhe hamaare liye kuchh lassi laane do." The roof did need fixing. The roof was old and shaggy, and I was starving. Some lassi would be enough to fill my stomach.

I went to the dining table and slumped down in the chair.

Moments later, Kajol auntie came into the room with a tray full of big, tall steel glasses. She called my mom and gave me a glass. I normally didn't like lassi because it tasted all weird and cold. But right now, I could drink the whole glass in a minute.

Once I finished with my lassi, I went up to the guest bedroom while mom fussed and talked and asked about the roof damage.

That was boring.
I sprang into the well-made bed with a rose-patterned soft blanket and light rose-pink-coloured pillows. The wall was a shade of baby pink, and the dressing table was covered with pink stuff. There was a picture of a rose, and there were two

vases filled with roses. The window was slightly open, letting warm air into the room. The sky was gray with clouds, but I could see little rays of sunlight peeking through. The window curtains were light pink. There was a small nightstand next to the bed. On the nightstand was a small normal lamp.

I guess this room was supposed to be full of pink. It looked cute if you looked at it the right way.

I spread out my arms and legs and stretched.

I grabbed my small pink and white rose bag. I guess it matches the room. I rolled over and pulled out my notebook with beautiful flowers and roses in a half pink, and a half black and white striped background.
I opened up to the middle and continued with my story. I had a gazillion ideas in my mind, and I felt like if I didn't write them all down, my head would explode.
My pencil tip hit the page from where I had left off, and I started scribbling down everything I could at once.

'On the beach, she tried to relax but couldn't stop crying. She couldn't find her brother or sister, and her younger brother was just sobbing and leaning against a rock. It wasn't helping either of them. Then the girl heard marching, and she got up, ran to her brother and told him to get up. Then, they both ran to the other end of the beach and beyond. They ran and ran. They ran until they reached the fields. They saw a small camp set up there with the country's flag printed on a tent.

'She and her brother ran to the tents, and a woman in white clothes came out and said they looked like they had been through a lot. The girl looked at herself to realize she was covered in blood and dirt. She looked at her brother and realized that he was covered in blood and dirt, too. The woman took them inside a large tent. The tent was filled with rows of beds filled with people who looked nastier than them. Then she asked the woman if her siblings had come here. The woman shook her head, got them settled in beds, and provided medical service.

'The girl stayed in the Medical Tent for two days, and her brother made a couple of friends who were in nearby beds. The girl looked around; every day, there would be more and more people lying on the beds with hideous and bloody injuries. She asked a nurse what was going on outside. The nurse said that the enemy had attacked all of our town and was moving towards the town near ours. The girl asked her where exactly they were. The nurse said they were in the valley. The girl had traveled a pretty long distance.

'The next day, she and her brother were given a small tent to live in. The tent was enough for now.'
I shook my hand. My hand was exhausted. I looked at my apple watch and realized that I only took thirty minutes to write this. It was 6:30 and it was getting dark. I rolled over. I wanted to write more, but I decided to take a small break.

I grabbed my pink and white rose bag and pulled out the book I needed to finish reading, Red Queen.

Red Queen was pretty interesting. I think I like it. I had to stop because Mom came into my room to call me down for dinner. I asked if Dad was home.

"He's thirty minutes from here."

I nodded and hurried downstairs.

"What were you doing up there for so long?" Mom asked.
"I wrote and wrote and wrote until my hand nearly died," I said.
All mom said was "hmm". I shrugged and then said, "And I was
reading, as you saw me doing that when you came in."

"Yes, yes…" she said in a bored and tired voice. Then she
looked around as if searching for hidden cameras as we
descended the stairs. "Who knew it could be so boring here?"

I snorted, and Mom let out a chuckle.

"Why? What'd you do?" I asked, knowing it was something
super boring.

"Nothing… We talked about Balwinder's new job and what
happened to the roof. Kajol looks as if she doesn't like talking,
but she talks so much," Mom blabbered on and on. "Good thing
that Balwinder went to get dad, or else. Who knew what would
have happened. I would have gone paagal." She would have
gone crazy. I know I would have gone crazy.

We made it down the stairs and went to the dining room.

"Ahh…What took you so long?" asked Kajol Auntie.
"Jaina wanted to finish her chapter," Mom said, making an
excuse.

Kajol shook her head and smiled.

"I made pav bhaji with garma, garma rotis," Kajol auntie squealed. Pav bhaji is like a gravy of blended vegetables with a bit of spicy spices. Pav bhaji is normally eaten with an Indian-style bread roll, but warm rotis or flatbread can replace the Pav. I licked my lips. It had been some time since Mom made this at home. I had always loved pav bhaji, and mom always gave it to me with butter. It tastes the best when it's all warm and fresh.

Once it's cold, you don't get the same taste from when it was fresh. I sat immediately waiting to dig in when Kajol auntie and mom stopped me at the same time. "Wash your hands first!" They both said in unison. Then, they laughed and I got up quickly and rushed down the hall to the bathroom. I turned on the faucet and freezing cold water came out. I didn't care. I squeezed some soap out from the soap bottle. I rubbed real quick then ran them under the faucet again until the little soap bubbles were gone. I rubbed my hands on my shirt and walked outside the bathroom to the dining room.

Chapter Thirteen

STORIES

I couldn't wait to dig into my pav bhaji.

The bhaji was hot, and bits of steam were blowing on my face. I quickly grabbed the roti, grabbed some of the bhaji, and plopped it into my mouth. It was so good!

I plopped onto my bed; I wasn't tired. I was bored. My head was filled with so many ideas for the small summary. I quickly grabbed my notebook and pencil and started scribbling stuff down.

I was still having trouble thinking of their names. I would have to do that later.

'One day, when the girl was wandering around the camp, she saw a huge crowd. She advanced forward carefully, knowing what had happened last time when she was in a huge crowd. She asked the man next to her what was happening there. The man said the prince was looking for a few people to take to the castle for the military and servants. The girl backed away; she didn't want to get chosen. She still had to find her older brother and sister, and she couldn't leave her younger brother.

'The girl ran back towards her tent, but then a guard stopped her. He forced her to turn around and go all the way in front of the crowd because she looked like a good maid. The girl screamed no, but the guard pointed the gun towards her. She had no choice but to go in front of the crowd. There, she saw the prince looking over the crowd. The prince caught the girl's gaze. The girl looked down.

'Then, a guard ordered her to come. She shook her head. The guard grabbed the girl's hand and pulled her forward. The girl screamed, but the guard dragged her anyway. The girl knew she was going to become a maid. She was taken into a beautiful white tent with the country's flag on it. She had tears in her eyes. Inside the tent, she saw a long bench with other girls on it. Their eyes were puffy, too. The girl knew what to do. The girl turned toward the guard that was holding her and bit his arm. He screamed in pain. The girl ran out of the tent, but more guards advanced on her. She saw a gun perched on the other tent walls. She didn't know how to use a gun, but she would figure it out later.

'Then the prince came running toward her, and she held the gun straight at the prince. She yelled to all the guards surrounding her, "STAND BACK, OR ELSE I WILL SHOOT YOUR BELOVED PRINCE!" The guards dropped their weapons and took a couple of steps back. The prince smirked and told the guards to leave and that he would manage on his own. The guards nodded and skittered away while the girl held the gun higher. The prince looked around and said that he wasn't there to harm her. The girl didn't believe that until… the prince fell to the ground unconscious. The girl looked over at the prince to see a small dart on the prince's neck.

'The girl gasped and then was about to make a run for it when another dart flew over her neck, and her eyes closed to pitch black.

'When the girl woke up, she found herself in a small carriage that was moving. She was still a little dizzy. It was a small type of carriage. There were small windows on the side with tiny curtains covering the window. The girl carefully moved the curtain away from the window. She looked outside the window, and her jaw hung open. A magnificent castle was standing tall, overlooking the big village. They were crossing the grand bridge with the gushing and glittering waterfall on the side. The girl had always heard stories about this place but never visited. Tall mountains and green forests stood behind the castle. The carriage continued until they reached the castle.
'When the carriage came to a halt, someone knocked on the carriage door. The girl was scared to come out, but she opened the door. There was a soldier standing there looking bored until he saw her. His mouth opened wide. The girl was confused. She came out of the carriage, the sunlight blinding her. Her hair, a tangled mess, blew softly. Last the girl remembered was when a dart pierced her neck, and she fell.

'The soldier pulled her out of the carriage and dragged her towards the castle. There were soldiers and guards everywhere. The girl was nearly terrified when she stopped in her tracks. The princess was looking down at them. The princess was super beautiful. The soldier hit the girl with his gun,, and the girl could feel hot blood trickling down her arm. The girl growled at the soldier.

'The girl and the soldier proceeded down the main hall and then into a more private room, which had four thrones placed in the middle. The thrones weren't the grand thrones from the throne room, but these thrones were smaller, and this room was more private.'

I couldn't stop writing. My hand was doing all the work. Surprisingly, my hand didn't hurt at all. I continued writing. 'All the royals were sitting in their own thrones. The soldier orders her to kneel, but the girl refuses. The soldier hit the girl in the leg, which forced her to kneel. She could feel a bruise forming there. The king talked to the girl about how she would become a maid at the palace. The queen said that she would have the princess teach the girl how to be a "lady". The girl shook her head, but the royals did not pay any attention to her. Once the girl and the royals finished talking, three maids walked in and escorted the girl into a large room with a large bed and beautiful decorations. The girl walked up to the mirror and laughed. In the mirror, she saw tangled hair, a bleeding lip, a small gash on her cheek with blood drooling out, two cuts on her arm, and her white shirt was half white, half covered with dirt.

'One of the maids came up to her and gave her a new set of clothes. The girl changed her clothes behind the curtains quickly. When she came out, the maids started untangling her hair, and one of them started putting some alcohol onto the girl's wounds. The girl groaned as the maid applied alcohol. Then, there was a knock on the door. Then the princess came out from the door. The maids immediately stopped what they were doing and bowed down in front of the princess. The girl just sat there, playing with her hands. The princess smiled and then laughed and laughed. The girl was confused about what the princess was laughing at. The princess managed to say that the girl had no manners. The girl just shrugged and told the maids to continue what they were doing.

'The princess was in utter shock. The girl asked what happened. The princess said that she was going to become a maid but the girl was treating herself as if she were the boss. The girl just responded, "gotta enjoy it when you can.'

Chapter Fourteen
A WONDERFUL IDEA

The sun shone brightly on my face as I stood there outside, getting ready to head back home. Such a relief to go back home. My parents had already loaded up the car with our luggage, and we were about to leave.

My parents waved to Balwinder uncle and Kajal's auntie as we climbed into the car. I was bored the moment I sat in my seat. I pulled out my notebook and my mechanical pencil. I tapped the pencil on my head, thinking of a good plot for the story.

'The princess said she liked the girl and might appoint her as her maid. The princess replied with ease and refused. The princess laughed, and the girl joined in. The next morning, there was a note on the girl's bedside table. The note told her to go down to breakfast with the royal family. The girl got dressed in white and normal pants and went to the breakfast room.'

I stopped; I was too bored. This always happens to me, and I hate it.

I didn't feel like writing right now, so I set aside my book and drifted into a long sleep.

I don't know what I saw in my dream, but it was weird. I was dreaming about the book summary that I was writing. I saw a girl in a beautiful white wedding dress. There was fresh blood smeared all over it. I would have considered it pretty if it wasn't for the blood.

The girl in the blood-stained wedding dress had her beautiful brown hair down, and she was carrying a blood-stained knife. A young man called out her name. She turned around.

Her face was horrifying and beautiful all the same. I loved it.

The girl's face had shining red blood splattered onto her face. The girl gasped, tears starting to form in her eyes. She ran faster and faster until she was in the man's arms. The girl muttered something like, "I thought you were dead."

The young man smiled and said, "I wouldn't want to miss my sister's wedding." The girl seemed to smile with her face buried in her brother's back. "What happened to your beautiful face?" The girl just shook her head. "I miss my mother too. How is she?" The girl stopped smiling and let go, backing away. The girl looked sad and wanted to cry. Her blood-stained face was not as scary as it was before. "She's gone, isn't she?"

Then, they heard gunshots and the girl turned and ran, taking her brother with her. They went on and on through small corridors until they reached a huge room that looked like a ball-room, or used to be a ball-room.

I woke up, happy that the dream had given me some help with my story. As soon I turned and looked out the window, I saw that we had just pulled into our driveway. Perfect timing.

EPILOGUE

I published four books over the time period of when I was in middle school to college. I found a genre that I love to write now.

Romance and thriller.

I love those two genres.

I ended up publishing the book, which I started in middle school in 8th grade.

I always wanted to write books with plot twists. I think I'm going to try writing that next, if I can think of a good plot twist.

Writing books is always a challenge. It's never easy.

I could never think of anything when I wanted to write a book.

I remember those times where I would just sit there and try to think. Sometimes, I tried to change the scenery to get a better idea on what to write.

My parents and family friends are supportive of being an author and I am glad and lucky.

Sometimes, writing helped me calm down when I was angry or depressed. Writing has a huge effect on my life. Writing is not easy, but I still enjoy it.

I used writing to write down special moments of my life, stories that came to mind, and more.

All I know is that I'm not going to quit writing, *ever*.

About the author

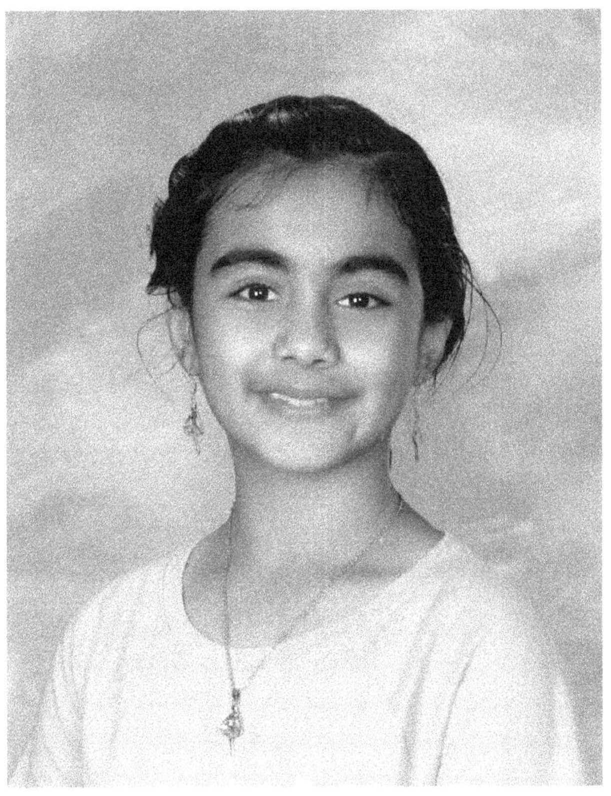

Kenisa Modi's journey as a writer began at a remarkably early age, sparked by a deep passion for storytelling and reading that started when she was just 4 years old. She resides in Mechanicsburg, Pennsylvania, with her family, where she spends her free time either engrossed in books or baking.

Verses Kindler Publication

Verses Kindler Publication

Reach us through our website -
https://www.verseskindlerpublication.com/
For more information visit our Instagram or Facebook page.